Corunity Learning & Libraries
Cymed Ddysgu a Llyfrgelloedd

Newport
CITY COUNCIL
CYNGOR DINAS
Casnewydd

This i should be returned or renewed by the
last dstamped below.

2 9 SEP 2021

2 0 JUN 2023

2 5 JUL 2023

To renew visit:

www.newport.gov.uk/libraries

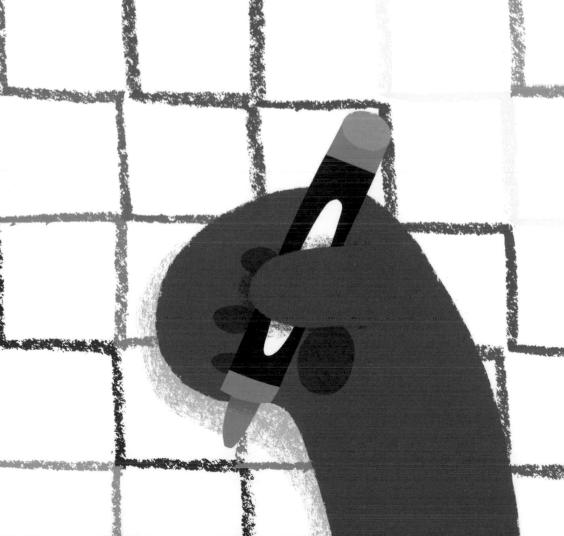

For Andrew: I love you any which way – **C. H.**

For Orson – **E. U.**

BLOOMSBURY CHILDREN'S BOOKS
Bloomsbury Publishing Plc
50 Bedford Square, London, WC1B 3DP, UK

BLOOMSBURY, BLOOMSBURY CHILDREN'S BOOKS and the Diana logo are trademarks of Bloomsbury Publishing Plc

First published in Great Britain by Bloomsbury Publishing Plc

Text copyright © Caryl Hart 2020
Illustrations copyright © Edward Underwood 2020

Caryl Hart and Edward Underwood have asserted their rights under the Copyright, Designs and Patents Act, 1988,
to be identified as the Author and Illustrator of this work

A catalogue record for this book is available from the British Library

ISBN 978 1 4088 9122 3 (HB)
ISBN 978 1 4088 9121 6 (PB)
ISBN 978 1 4088 9123 0 (eBook)

1 3 5 7 9 10 8 6 4 2

Printed and bound in China by Leo Paper Products, Heshan, Guangdong
All papers used by Bloomsbury Publishing Plc are natural, recyclable products from wood grown in well managed forests.
The manufacturing processes conform to the environmental regulations of the country of origin.

To find out more about our authors and books visit www.bloomsbury.com and sign up for our newsletters

BEARS LOVE SQUARES

Written by

Caryl Hart

Illustrated by

Edward Underwood

BLOOMSBURY
CHILDREN'S BOOKS

LONDON   OXFORD   NEW YORK   NEW DELHI   SYDNEY

Shapes are all around us.

We see them **everywhere**.

But bears are
very choosy . . .

BEARS love SQUARES!

Squares are nice and even. Their corners are just so.

Squares are always just the **same** any way they go.

But what about
these **rectangles**?
Their sides are
straight and long.

Their corners are
all cornery.

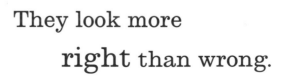

They look more
right than wrong.

LOOK! They're *almost* like a square –
just give a little squeeze . . .

Come on, Bear.

Check this out!

Won't you **try** one?

Please?

I hear what you are saying
    but I really do not care.
Those sides are still too long and thin
    and . . .

BEARS love SQUARES!

How about **triangles**?
They're so
tremendous, see?

They tip
and
flip
three different ways.

And
corners?

They have THREE.

This triangle's a mountain –
climb up and see
the view . . .

Won't you have a triangle?
Come on, try something new!

This will NOT do. No, not at all.

I don't like mountain air.

Your triangle's far too pointy

and . . .

BEARS love
SQUARES!

Well, circles are sensational.

They have no points at all.

Come, have some fun with circles –
we both could have a ball!

Circles can be **friendly**.
Circles are such fun . . .

I'm **sure** you'd like a circle.
Why don't you try
this one?

I would NOT like a circle.
I'm sure I do not dare.
Your circles are TOO curvy
and . . .

BEARS love
SQUARES!

There **must** be something in this box.
I'll see what I can **find**.

There **has** to be some sort of shape
to help you **change** your mind.

This **pentagon** has FIVE sides.

This **hexagon** has SIX.

But, hang on . . .

Here's a **star** shape.
Let's throw this in the mix.

Please STOP this silly nonsense.
I'm tearing out my hair.
I'll say it clearly
ONE more time . . .

BEARS love SQUARES!

Just **try** this final
little **thing?**

A shape . . .

Made just for YOU!

Now that's a shape . . .
I DO like.

I LOVE IT,
yes I do!

(But I still like
squares too.)